NICK JR

DORA the EXPLORER™

Scavenger Hunt

Little Look and Find™

Illustrated by Bob Roper

Published by
Louis Weber, C.E.O., Publications International, Ltd.
7373 North Cicero Avenue, Lincolnwood, Illinois 60712

Ground Floor, 59 Gloucester Place, London W1U 8JJ

Customer Service: 1-800-595-8484 or customer_service@pilbooks.com

www.pilbooks.com

Little Look and Find is a trademark of
Publications International, Ltd.
p i kids is a registered trademark
of Publications International, Ltd.
Look and Find is a registered trademark
of Publications International, Ltd.,
in the United States and in Canada.

8 7 6 5 4 3 2 1

ISBN-13: 978-1-4127-7113-9
ISBN-10: 1-4127-7113-7

¡Hola! I'm Dora. Today in school, my teacher Maestra Beatriz gave us a homework project. It's a scavenger hunt! The scavenger hunt starts here in my classroom. I need to find something that starts with each letter of the alphabet. Will you help me?

LION

ZEBRA

Boots is going to help us with the scavenger hunt, too! Let's find these things on the playground.

one slide
un resbalón

two seesaws
dos balancines

four bicycles
cuatro bicicletas

three swings
tres columpios

five sand castles
*cinco castillos
de arena*

seven bats
siete bates

six mitts
*seis guantes
de beisbol*

eight baseballs
ocho beisbols

nine soccer balls
nueve fútbols

ten marbles
diez canicas

Where can we find the rest of the things on the scavenger hunt list? Let's ask Map! Help us match the places we need to go with the pictures on Map.

Benny's Barn

Tico's Workshop

Isa's Garden

Mucky Mud

Shape Forest

Next on our scavenger hunt list are shapes. We can look for them in Shape Forest! Will you help us find these shapes?

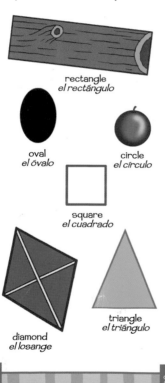

rectangle
el rectángulo

oval
el óvalo

circle
el círculo

square
el cuadrado

diamond
el losange

triangle
el triángulo

Now we need to find things that go! Tico always has lots of those. Will you come with us to look for these things at Tico's Workshop in the Nutty Forest?

car
el coche

airplane
el avión

motorcycle
la motocicleta

wagon
la carreta

balloon
el globo

rowboat
el bote

We want to go to Isa's Flowery Garden, but first we need to cross the Mucky Mud! Can you find these items that will help us get across?

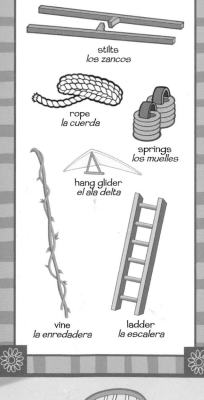

stilts
los zancos

rope
la cuerda

springs
los muelles

hang glider
el ala delta

vine
la enredadera

ladder
la escalera

We've made it to Isa's Flowery Garden! Next on the scavenger hunt list are colors. Let's find a flower for each color.

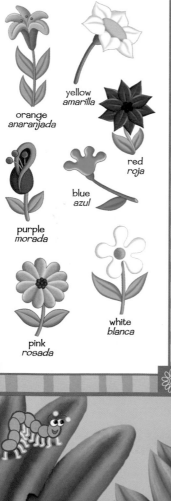

orange
anaranjada

yellow
amarilla

red
roja

blue
azul

purple
morada

white
blanca

pink
rosada

We're almost done with the scavenger hunt. I just need to find these farm animals. Will you help me look for them at Benny's Barn?

cow
la vaca

pig
el cerdo

duck
el pato

goat
la cabra

sheep
el carnero

chicken
el pollo

horse
el caballo

The fun's not over yet!
Go back to each scene
and search for these
hidden surprises.

The Playground

Search for these numbers
on the playground:

☐ 1   ☐ 4
☐ 2   ☐ 5
☐ 3

Dora's Classroom

Find these things that will
help Dora practice writing
the alphabet:

☐ pencil
☐ pen
☐ crayon
☐ piece of chalk
☐ marker

Mucky Mud

Watch out for that sneaky
fox, Swiper, while you search
for these things that rhyme
with fox:

☐ socks   ☐ rocks
☐ box   ☐ blocks

Map

Locate these other places and objects on Map:

- [ ] tree
- [ ] rock
- [ ] stream
- [ ] mountain
- [ ] house

Shape Forest

Stars are shapes! See if you can find these stars:

- [ ] purple star
- [ ] blue star
- [ ] red star
- [ ] yellow star
- [ ] white star

Tico's Workshop

Revisit Tico's Workshop and try to find these other things that go:

- [ ] bicycle
- [ ] pair of roller skates
- [ ] skateboard
- [ ] tricycle
- [ ] sled

Isa's Flowery Garden

Find these other colorful things in the garden:

- [ ] rainbow
- [ ] paints
- [ ] crayons
- [ ] balloons

Benny's Barn

Look for these other animals:

- [ ] cat
- [ ] dog
- [ ] mouse
- [ ] rabbit
- [ ] fish